Reycraft Books
55 Fifth Avenue
New York, NY 10003

Reycraftbooks.com

Reycraft Books is a trade imprint and trademark of Newmark Learning, LLC.

This edition is published by arrangement with China Children's Press & Publication Group Co., Ltd.
© China Children's Press & Publication Group Co., Ltd.
English translation provided by China Children's Press & Publication Group Co., Ltd.

Library of Congress Control Number: 2021914496

ISBN: 978-1-4788-7524-6

Printed in Dongguan, China. 8557/0721/18155

10 9 8 7 6 5 4 3 2 1

First Edition Hardcover published by Reycraft Books 2021.

My Dragon Boat Festival

Written by Bing Ge
Illustrated by Li Li

It's a family tradition for my
mom and dad to take me back to our
hometown for the Dragon Boat Festival. We pack
all our bags and travel by train, boat, and bus. The best
part of the journey is meandering the country roads. There
are always wild flowers blooming in the tall grasses
and water buffaloes working in the rice
paddies.

After walking across the stone bridge and through the flagstone streets, we're happy to find Grandma and Grandpa waiting, their little spotted dog gleefully wagging its tail.

We have brought gifts from the city to share.
My mom says to Grandma, "I chose this
fine cloth coat especially for you.
You can wear it to go dancing!"

Grandma's smile is huge.
"It's so colorful! Thank you for such a thoughtful gift."

"That's a beautiful coat. You'll look
lovely in it," says Grandpa.

Dad gives a box of vacuum-packed zongzi to Grandpa. "I brought this for us to eat during the Dragon Boat Festival."

Grandpa laughs. "While you're here, you'll be treated to homemade zongzi!"

In the kitchen, I see small bowls filled with lotus seeds, soy beans, red beans, peanuts, red dates, candied dates, raisins, and sweetened bean paste. Next to them is a bucket of sticky rice that has been soaked in water.

These are all the ingredients for zongzi.

"We use only the freshest leaves to make
the zongzi," Grandpa says proudly.
"Come with me to pick some!"

Rowing the boat, Grandpa hums softly.
Following his lead, Dad and I start to sing.

Pick the reed leaves.
Pick the reed leaves.
The green reed leaves are shiny and long.

Soon, our basket is full of them.

Arriving home, I plead with Grandma,
"Let's make some zongzi!"

We gather all the ingredients
and wash the reed leaves.

Sitting in a circle, we begin making
the special treat. Grandma forms each leaf
into a little bowl and Mom and I scoop in
the zongzi mixture before tying it up.

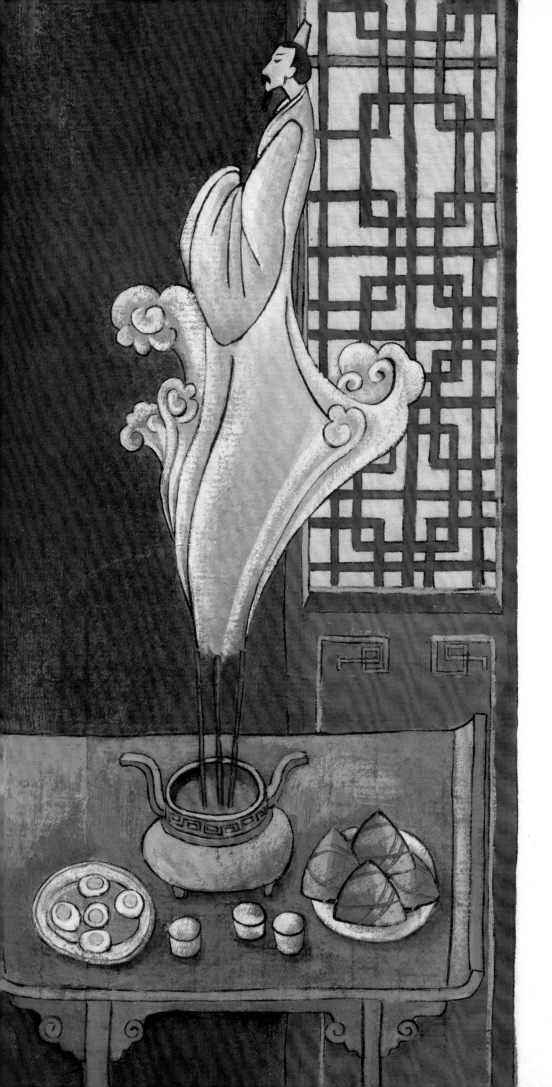

I tell Grandma, "Our teacher taught us that our ancestors founded the Dragon Boat Festival to honor the patriotic poet Qu Yuan."

"That's right," Grandma says with a smile. "The dragon boat race is also in his honor."

The zongzi boil in a big pot over the fire. I help Grandma fan the flames and get soot on my face.

When the zongzi are finally done, I am dying to try them all. There is nothing more delicious than homemade zongzi!

As she tucks me in that night, Grandma says,

"Tomorrow morning, I'll show you some 50-year-old zongzi."

How is it possible for zongzi to be so old?

When I wake up the next morning, the house is full of colorful decorations made to look like zongzi. There's also a picture of Grandma from her childhood. In it, she has pigtails and wears a colorful mini-zongzi necklace made from silk thread. That's what she meant when she talked about the 50-year-old zongzi. They are so beautiful!

After seeing the photo, I want to learn to make mini-zongzi
out of silk thread. "Please, please teach me!" I beg Grandma.
"I want to make some for my friends."

Hearing this, Grandma takes my hand and patiently shows me.
Quick as can be, we make a dozen mini-zongzi.

Then, like a magician, Grandma creates different shaped sachets.
She puts the most beautiful one around my neck. "When we
were kids, we would wear sachets during the Dragon Boat
Festival. They're not just beautiful—they also ward off evil."

"Has Grandpa ever worn one?" I suddenly realize that I haven't seen him since morning. "Where is he, anyway?"

Dad beams. "Grandpa is preparing for the dragon boat race. Let's go and watch him!"

Gongs and drums signal people to start gathering near the river. Several dragon boats are lined up along the riverbank. What an impressive scene!

Grandpa is wearing his dragon boat rowing suit with a yellow bandana tied around his head. He looks so handsome!

"Your grandpa has been the helmsman for decades," Dad says proudly.

The dragon boat race begins. Grandpa sits at the front of the boat, beating his drum vigorously.

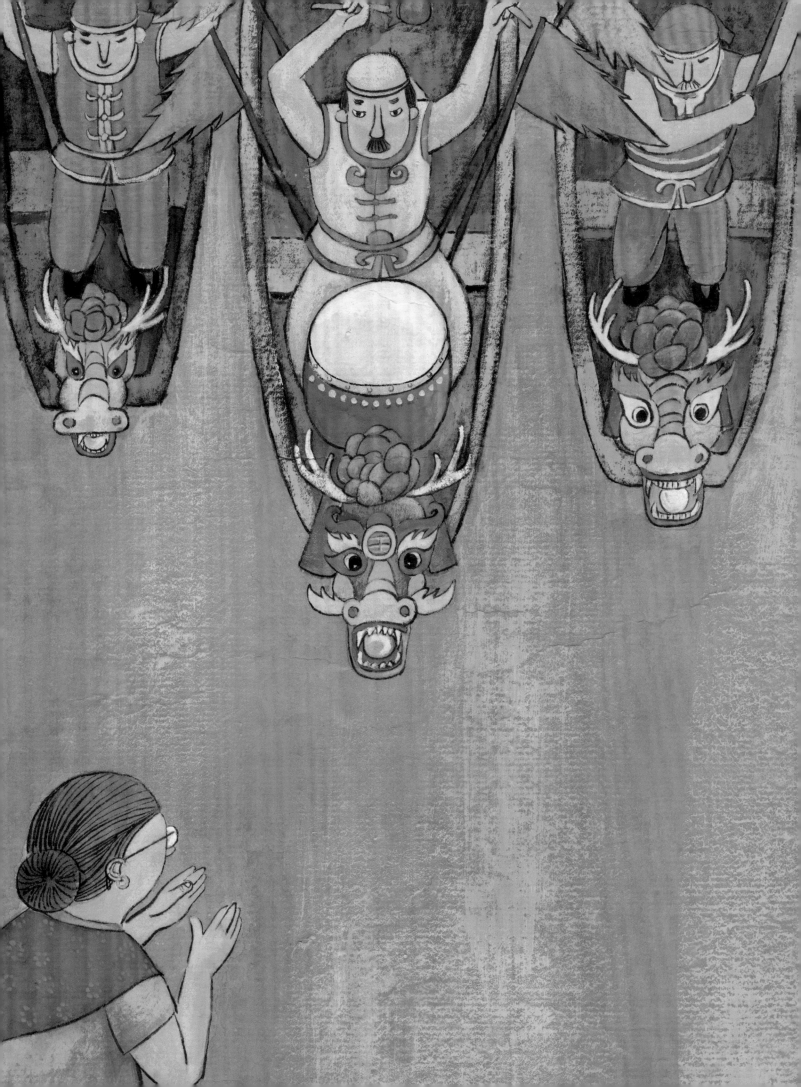

Grandpa's team is the first to cross the finish line.
Grandma can't help but glow with pride and admiration.

Grandpa's dragon boat rowing suit is so cool!
"I'd like to try it on," I say.

The suit is much too big for me.
Still, people smile and tell me I look nice in it.

Soon, the Dragon Boat Festival is over and we head home to the city. We get back on the bus, the boat, and the train, loaded down with gifts to share with friends.

I had so much fun. I can't wait to come back for the festival again next year!

The Dragon Boat Festival

by Yongyi Yue
PhD in Folklore, Beijing Normal University, and
Director of the Beijing Folk Artists Association

The Origin of the Dragon Boat Festival

Like the Spring Festival, Mid-Autumn Festival, and Qingming Festival, the Dragon Boat Festival on the fifth day of the fifth lunar month is one of the most important festivals in the ancient Chinese festival system. The Dragon Boat Festival has many other names, such as the May Festival, the Zongzi Festival, the Poet's Festival, and the Girl's Festival. It is one of the traditional Chinese festivals with the most names. There are many theories about the origin of the Dragon Boat Festival. Today, one of the most widely held theories is that the festival began as a way to commemorate the great poet Qu Yuan.

Dragon Boat Festival Traditions

The fifth month of the lunar calendar is also known as the "evil month," so the Dragon Boat Festival has a series of rituals designed to eliminate pests, poison, and evil. On the day of the Dragon Boat Festival, people tie charms in front of their doors, put wormwood on their doors and windows, put swords and peach branches on their beds, bathe in orchid soup, and put sachets on children.

Rice Dumplings and Dragon Boats

Zongzi, also called squash rice dumplings or tube dumplings, are a traditional holiday food for the Dragon Boat Festival. Zongzi are usually made by wrapping glutinous rice with bamboo, rue, or reed leaves (or putting the rice in bamboo tubes), adding other fillings, and steaming them. Zongzi are mostly shaped like pyramids.

Dragon boat racing is one of the most important activities of the Dragon Boat Festival. A dragon boat is a boat painted with a dragon pattern or shaped like a dragon. Dragon boat racing is a traditional Chinese water sport and entertainment in which multiple people can participate.

Girl's Day

For women, the Dragon Boat Festival is a special festival, because the Dragon Boat Festival is also known as "Girl's Day." As early as the Ming dynasty, from the first day to the fifth day of the fifth month of the lunar calendar, every household in Beijing would use pomegranate flowers to make little girls look beautiful, and their married daughters would also return home.

Bing Ge

is a member of the Chinese Writer's Association. He is the author of the short story collection "Green Cat," which won the Second National Outstanding Children's Literature Award. He has also published numerous award-winning fairy tales.

Li Li

was born in Hangzhou, China, and graduated from the China Academy of Art. She currently teaches at the Children's Art Education Department of Hangzhou Preschool Teachers College, Zhejiang Normal University. Her award-winning works have been selected for the National Art Exhibition numerous times.